TREETOP TWINS
WILDERNESS ADVENTURES

The Twins Meet
a Quagga

Cressida Cowell

Hodder
Children's
Books

There are eight butterflies in this
book. Can you find them all?

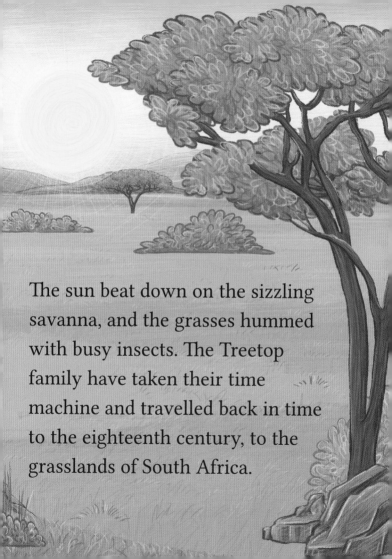

The sun beat down on the sizzling savanna, and the grasses hummed with busy insects. The Treetop family have taken their time machine and travelled back in time to the eighteenth century, to the grasslands of South Africa.

One bright blue day, the big twins, Alfie and Asha, were looking after the little twins, Tulip and Ted. Their parents, Professor Pablo and Professor Penelope, were taking a nap.

When the professors woke up, the Treetop family were going to spend the evening at a nearby waterhole, to see what animals were living in the African savanna at that time.

'There'll be cheetahs...' said Asha.

'And ostriches,' said Alfie.

'And lions and elephants,' said Ted.

'Don't forget the unicorns!' said Tulip.

'Don't be silly!' laughed Ted. 'Only babies believe in unicorns!'

Alfie and Asha were laughing too, which made Tulip very upset.

'I'll show them I'm not a baby!' said Tulip to herself. 'I'll go down to the waterhole and look for unicorns on my own...'

So when the others weren't
looking, Tulip decided to walk
to the waterhole by herself.
She found a hill to hide behind,
and ducked down out of sight.
From her hiding place, she spotted
an ostrich, and a wildebeest, and...

a herd of creatures she had never
seen before!

Tulip couldn't see them properly,
because there were some trees in
the way. From the side, they looked
a little bit like horses, but they were
much smaller, so they must be...

'Unicorns!' said Tulip triumphantly. 'I knew it!'

Meanwhile, Alfie and Asha and Ted had noticed that Tulip was missing. They woke up Professor Penelope and Professor Pablo, and they all hurried to the waterhole.

They crept up very quietly so as not to disturb the animals and peered over Tulip's shoulder.

'I'm sorry I called you a baby,' whispered Ted.

'And I'm sorry I ran off without telling you where I was going,' whispered Tulip. 'But look! I did find some unicorns...'

Just then one of the strange creatures turned towards them. And it did not have a horn.

'Oh!' said Tulip, feeling very disappointed. 'It isn't a unicorn after all!'

But it did have something else interesting. It had stripes! But not all over it – just on its front half.

'It's a quagga,' said Professor Penelope. 'It's about the size of a zebra, but with stripes only on the front half of its body.'

'Why is it called a quagga?' asked Tulip.

The quagga opened up its mouth and made a noise – 'KWA-GA!'

'That must be why!' grinned Ted.

But the quagga had made that noise for a reason.

There were three beautiful, golden lionesses padding towards the waterhole!

The lionesses prowled closer. But the quaggas had already been alerted. 'KWA-GA!' they cried as they all ran away.

All except for one...a baby, who couldn't run quite fast enough.

'Oh no!' cried Tulip. 'They're going to catch it!'

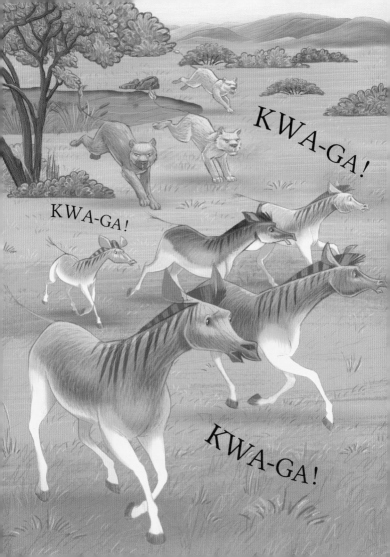

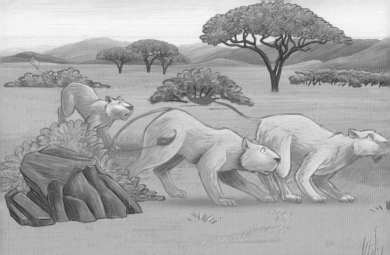

But then something amazing
happened.

A great big wildebeest saw the
baby quagga was in trouble.
It stepped forward and shook its
enormous horns at the lionesses.

The lionesses were scared, and
now it was their turn to run away.

'Phew!' said Alfie. 'Why did
that big wildebeest save the baby
quagga?'

'We ALL have to look after the
babies, even if they aren't ours,'
said Asha, putting her arm
around Tulip.

'I'M not a baby,' said Tulip,

but she smiled and hugged Asha anyway.

And then the Treetop family walked back home through the cooling grass for dinner.

Night-time in the savanna. Professor Pablo was putting the twins to bed.

'I'm so glad we got to travel back in time and meet the quaggas,' said Asha, who had drawn a picture of one in her notebook.

'Me too,' said Professor Pablo, turning the light off. 'Sorry it wasn't a unicorn, Tulip – but it was almost as good!'

'I wonder what year and what place we'd have to travel to to see a unicorn?' said Tulip to herself. 'One day I'll find a unicorn, just you wait and see!'

ASHA'S FACTS ABOUT QUAGGAS

The quagga was about the size of a zebra, but only had stripes on the front half of its body.

Quaggas lived up until the late nineteenth century on the plains of South Africa.

'The Quaggas' name may have come from the noise they made - Kwa-Ga!